AF580253

THIS BOOK BELONGS TO:

FROM:

Published 2021
by Homeschool Social Enterprise Ltd
49 Manifold Way,
Wednesbury,
Sandwell
WS10 0GB

This book has been typeset in Comic Neue regular.

Printed in the United Kingdom.

ISBN 978-0-9957672-3-2

www.mawuenarankine.com

ACKNOWLEDGEMENTS

Special thanks:

To YAHWEH (GOD), for providing the skills and resources for this project, You are everything.

To my husband for always encouraging me.

To my son for inspiring me to reach beyond.

To my parents who nurtured and never gave up on me.

To my grandparents for their sacrifice.

To my siblings who continue to raise the bar.

To my nephews and nieces who carry the baton.

To my family and friends who have become family for bringing reason to each day.

To my aunt for taking the time to proofread and support.

Thoughts and prayers also go out to the homeless and 'hidden' population. With faith and love, you can overcome.

I love you all.

DANA'S NOT-SO-ORDINARY DAY

Written, illustrated and edited by
Mawuena Rankine

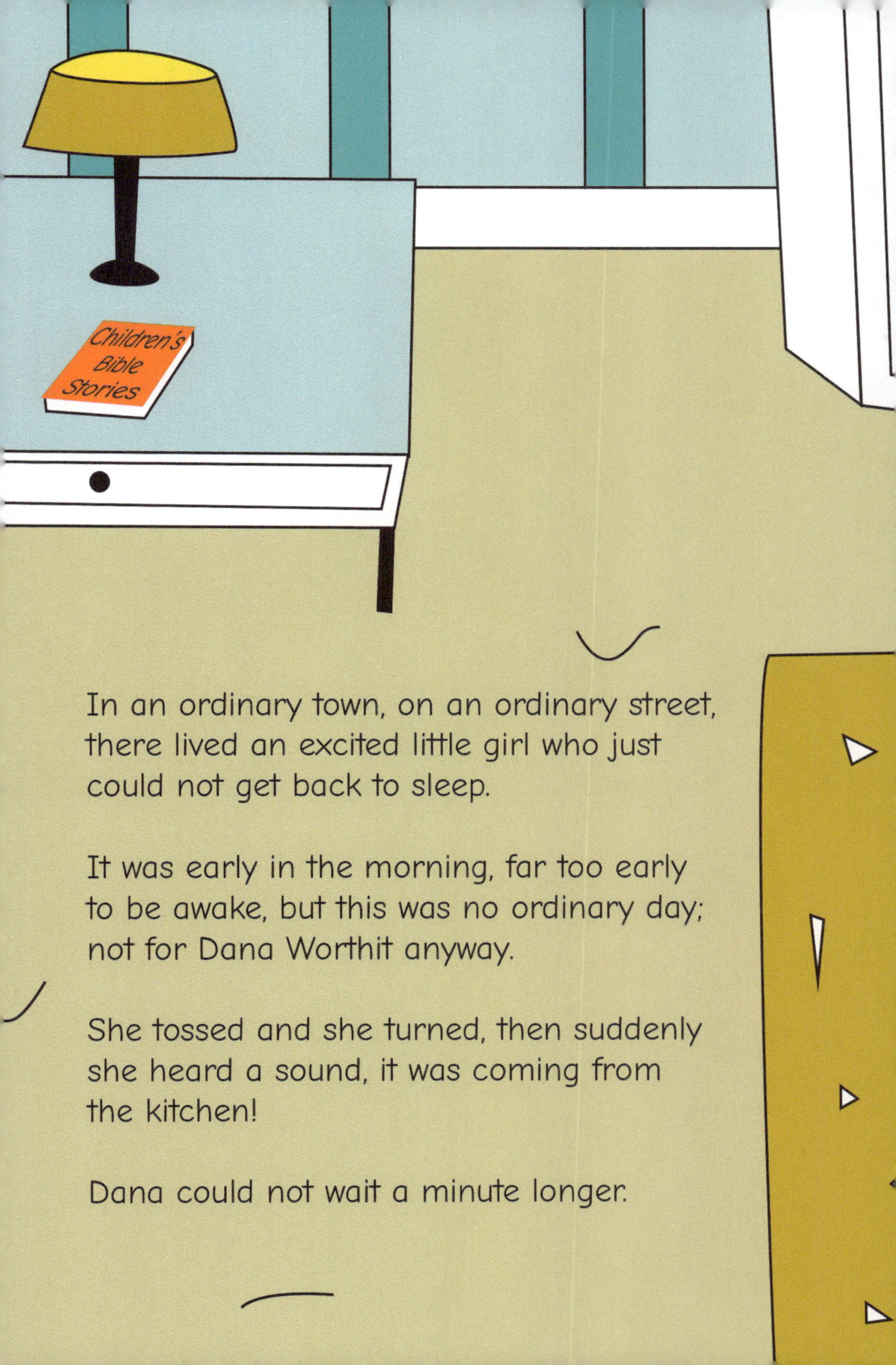

In an ordinary town, on an ordinary street, there lived an excited little girl who just could not get back to sleep.

It was early in the morning, far too early to be awake, but this was no ordinary day; not for Dana Worthit anyway.

She tossed and she turned, then suddenly she heard a sound, it was coming from the kitchen!

Dana could not wait a minute longer.

Saltfish
Ackee
Ackee

She jumped out of bed and headed downstairs. As she opened the kitchen door, there stood Dad, chopping up onions.

"Morning DD" he said, "you're up early."

Dad was making breakfast, but no ordinary breakfast, he was cooking up a delicious Caribbean feast!

There was ackee and saltfish, flour for the dumplings, plantain and even tasty avacado, yuuuummmyyy.

Dad and Dana had a wonderful time preparing breakfast and tidying up. They made the perfect tag team.

Soon, the whole family was wide awake and connected in the kitchen, when, the doorbell rang.

FAITH
HOPE
LOVE

It was the first day of summer break and for the Worthit family, that could only mean one thing...

"Grandma! Grandad! You're here!" Dana squealed.

Dana just loved seeing her grandparents. They were sooo much fun and full of wonderful surprises.

They talked and they ate and they talked some more. Grandad was a great storyteller, but Grandma always had the best jokes.

After breakfast, once everyone was nice and full, Grandad pulled out a card. “Here Princess,” he said, handing the card to Dana.

Dana looked at the card with curiosity. She had no idea what it could be for.

£20
To Dana,
Congratulations
for becoming The Outstanding
Achiever at school.
We knew you could do it!
Love always,
Grandad + Grandma
xxx

Last week, Dana received her school's highest award – 'The Outstanding Achiever' award.

"Thank you so much!" she said to her grandparents, excitedly. "Now I can buy my skates!"

Dana was learning to save her money. Recently, she had been saving up to buy the Skater 3000s, a pair of roller skates that she had seen advertised in a magazine.

Dad had taken the day off work and so the whole family decided to go into Town. There was always plenty to do and see there.

Dana definitely liked this idea. Now that she had enough savings, today was the perfect chance to buy her roller skates!

At last, they arrived. They parked their cars and headed towards Toy World, the biggest toy shop in Town.

The elders paced slowly behind Mum, whilst Dad and Baby Kwabena took the lead.

FREE CASH WI
HOMELESS,
PLEASE
HELP

TOY WORLD

Dana stood outside the shop for some time, but she did not go inside.

"I've changed my mind," she said eventually. "Can I buy something else instead?"

Everyone looked puzzled, but her parents agreed with her decision. After all, she had worked so hard to save her own money.

Dana walked into the supermarket next door. She picked up a basket and filled it with all of her favourite foods.

The adults were even more confused, but it was not every day that Dana got the chance to shop, so Dad allowed her to continue.

The family had a great time in Town. Grandad and Grandma visited their favourite shops and Dana continued to buy little treats, adding them to her collection.

Later on, Dad decided to buy everyone a tasty milkshake. Dana enjoyed this very much, but she was also eager to get back to the car.

On the way back, Dana stopped.

Earlier, she had noticed a man sitting on the pavement with a sign.

The poor man was still there.

"Can I help him Dad?" asked Dana.

"Yes," said Dad.

So Dana walked with Dad to hand over her bag of shopping.

"Here you go," she said to the man, "I bought this for you."

The man looked at Dana and was very grateful. "Thank you little one," he said with tears of joy.

"I'm glad you can see me. It's nice to know that I'm not invisible."

The adults were shocked, but very pleased with Dana. They all knew just how much she wanted those skates, but instead she chose to help someone in need.

When the family got home, Dad and Grandad relaxed and the children played while Mum finally opened the mail. This left Grandma to cook her special dish.

Not long after dinner, Dana and Kwabena were feeling sleepy. It had been a long day.

DANA

Dana said goodnight and went to her room to get ready for bed, but to her surprise, there was a parcel waiting for her.

In the end, it was fair to say, that Dana had an extraordinary day.

ALWAYS ASK A PARENT OR GUARDIAN FOR PERMISSION AND HELP BEFORE YOU GIVE A DONATION TO A HOMELESS PERSON.

LEARNING QUESTIONS

1. Why was Dana excited in the morning?

___

2. Which grandparent is funnier?

___

3. What award did Dana receive from school?

___

4. Why did Dana stand outside the toy shop for so long?

___

5. When did Dana's skates arrive?

___

6. Why do you think the homeless man said 'it's nice to know that I'm not invisible.'?

___

7. What could be the moral of this story?

___

About the author

Me (around Dana's age) Me now

Mawuena Rankine is a Christian Author, a wife, a mother and campaigner for the homeless amongst other marginalised groups.

These experiences led her to the idea of Dana's character and story.

Mawuena used her childhood passion for art and literature to illustrate, write and edit this book with the hope that it will teach and inspire children for generations to come.

Dear parents and guardians:
Join the community today as we share the story and highlight the issue of homelessness together. Use the hashtags **#danasnotsoordinaryday #theworthits and #endhomelessness** when sharing social media posts about the book. Also visit: **www.mawuenarankine.com**

May God bless you, peace be with you and I thank you for your support. Proverbs 22:6

1. She knew her grandparents were due to visit. 2. Grandma. 3. The Outstanding Achiever. 4. She was deciding what to do.
5. In the morning by the postman when her grandparents arrived. 6. Because other people walked past without helping him.
7. Example: When you do good, good things happen to you.

www.ingramcontent.com/pod-product-compliance
Lightning Source LLC
LaVergne TN
LVHW021315160826
845679LV00001B/364

9780995767232